To Holly, who helped, and to Scott—P.M.

To Vincent, our beautiful baby boy—B.T.

First published in the United States by
Phyllis Fogelman Books
An imprint of Penguin Putnam Books for Young Readers
345 Hudson Street
New York, New York 10014
Published in Great Britain by Frances Lincoln Limited
Text copyright © 2003 by Penny McKinlay
Illustrations copyright © 2003 by Britta Teckentrup
All rights reserved
Text set in Jacoby
Manufactured in Singapore

1 3 5 7 9 10 8 6 4 2

Library of Congress Cataloging-in-Publication Data
McKinlay, Penny.
Bumposaurus / Penny McKinlay ; illustrated by Britta Teckentrup.
p.   cm.
Summary: When a little brontosaurus keeps falling and bumping into
things, his mother thinks he is the adventurous type, but his
grandmother discovers the real reason.
ISBN 0-8037-2898-0
[1. Apatosaurus—Fiction. 2. Dinosaurs—Fiction.
3. Eyeglasses—Fiction.] I. Teckentrup, Britta. II. Title.
PZ7.M4786783 Bu 2003   [E]—dc21

BUMPOSAURUS

Penny McKinlay

Illustrated by **Britta Teckentrup**

PHYLLIS FOGELMAN BOOKS 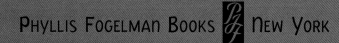 NEW YORK

There was once a baby dinosaur who was so nearsighted, he couldn't find his way out of his egg.

BUMP! BUMP!

BUMP!

he went inside the shell.

At last his mother heard him bumping and helped him out. "I think we'll call you Bumposaurus!" she said.

Bumposaurus ran off straight past his brothers and sisters.
He ran over the edge of the sandy hollow,
he fell down a very steep hill,

and he landed in a very **deep**

bog.

"Mother!" called the other baby dinosaurs. "Bumpy's stuck!"
Mother hauled him out, licking the mud lovingly off his nose. "He's
obviously the adventurous type!" she said to Father.

"Come and play tag, Bumpy!" cried his brothers
and sisters. "You're IT!" And they ran off giggling.
     Bumposaurus **s t r e t c h e d** his long neck
this way and that.
     "Where are you?" he called.

"We're over here!" they cried,
creeping closer.
Still he couldn't see them.

"Here!" they cried, creeping
closer still.

"Oh, there you are!" cried Bumposaurus.
He swung around suddenly and knocked
them down like bowling pins.

BUMP!

BUMP!

BUMP!

Mother gave them each a loving lick.
"Lunchtime!" she said.

Lunch was leaves. Lunch was always leaves.
"Not leaves again," moaned the babies.
"Now children," scolded their father.
"You know we Brontosauruses don't believe
in eating other dinosaurs!"

Bumposaurus began to munch obediently
on what lay before him.

It turned out to be his sister's tail.

"Father!" she shrieked. "Bumpy's eating me!"
"Bumposaurus!" said Father sternly.
"Eating dinosaurs is wrong!"

After lunch, Bumposaurus
went off to explore.

Bump!

His head hit something hard.
He looked up. The something
stretched high above him.

"Sorry, Father," he said. "I didn't see you."

Father said nothing.

"I know you're cross about me eating Bella. I didn't mean to."

Still Father said nothing.

"You see, Father, I think there's something wrong with me. I feel as though I'm different from the others."

And he poured out the whole story.

But Father still
said nothing.
He couldn't,
because in fact
he was a
tree.

"Oh, well," sighed Bumposaurus. "If you're that angry, I'll have to leave home."
And he set off.

Bumposaurus came to the edge of a wide river. "Lucky these logs are here. I don't have to get my feet wet."

"What a hot day it is!

"Funny . . . there doesn't seem to be anybody else around!"

By now Bumposaurus felt like
giving up and going home.
He was covered in bumps.
He was tired and lonely and
longing for a loving lick from Mother.
At last he stumbled into a sandy hollow.

"Home!"

he cried in joy.

And he snuggled up cozily
and fell asleep . . .

next to a **very large** Tyrannosaurus Rex.

The Tyrannosaurus was sleeping off a heavy meal, most definitely not of leaves! He was surprised when he woke to find a small Brontosaurus fast asleep in his nest.

"yum!" he said, and gave Bumpy an experimental lick.

"You're not my mother," yelped Bumpy, waking up with a jump.

"no, but you're my **dessert!"**

And the Tyrannosaurus grinned
a horrible grin, bristling with
razor-sharp teeth.

But just at that moment there came the thunderous sound of forty galloping feet. Ten furious Brontosaurus faces glared into the hollow.

"put my son down!"

bellowed Father.

"Eating dinosaurs is wrong!"

"Quite right, quite right!"
the Tyrannosaurus said quickly.
"What was I thinking of?
Please excuse me!"
   And he ran off.

When Bumposaurus got home, his mother gave him
the most loving lick ever. "Say hello to Grandma,
Bumposaurus," she said.

"Where?"

said Bumposaurus.

"Here," said a gentle voice, and a soft and wrinkled face
bent close to his. "Now you can see me, can't you?" she said.

"What are those circles around your eyes, Grandma?"
asked Bumpy.

"Try them on, and see, little one," she said.

Bumposaurus slid the glasses onto his nose. At once, a wonderful world of *smiling* faces leaped out at him.

At last he could see!